Night Life

A Rural Folk Horror Field Guide

Alba V Sarria

Praise for Night Life

"Lyric prose weaving into the shape of beasts— the reason your Appalachian mamaw tells you not to look into the woods after dark. For everyone who has ever loved a monster and prayed it would love you back. Absolutely beautiful."
—**Andrew Joseph White,** *New York Times* **Bestselling author of** *HELL FOLLOWED WITH US* **and** *THE SPIRIT BARES ITS TEETH*

"*NIGHT LIFE* is folk horror distilled down to its rawest, most primal element: a *knowing* that doesn't exist outside the backwoods, byways, and those places forgotten by time and feared by man. There is love and death and worship bound up in Sarria's quietly fierce poetry. Bloody and haunting, this collection is perfect for anyone who hears whispers in the forest, feels eyes on them in the night, or shies away from dark waters' touch."
—**Siggy Chambers, author of** *THE BINDING OF BLOOM MOUNTAIN*

"Haunting, intricate, and steeped in rich folklore. Sarria weaves an intoxicating fever dream of a tale that will leave you hungry for more."
—**Sophia Slade, bestselling author of** *NIGHTSTRIDER* **and** *VALKYRIE*

Published by Monstrous Love Lounge Press

ISBN 979-8-218-28888-4

Second Edition, 2024

10 9 8 7 6 5 4 3 2 1

Cover art by Grim Poppy Designs

Internal illustrations by M.E Morgan

For my beloved husband—

Thank you for all those 3AM graveyard dates and 8hr deep-night drives through twisting lone mountain roads that had our eyes finding hauntings, Old Gods, and love in the dark. You are my pomegranate tree in the desert

Contents

Marked

Avert All Mortal Eyes

Awaken

Introduction

Neighbor

He stands at the far end of the living room;
body lithe,
twisted
narrow.

My mind confuses Him for a tree; all
gnarled and knobby.
           Bent back grazing the
           low ceiling,
           Head hanging
           like dry rotted fruit
           with pinprick maggot-white
           eyes
           that follow me
           from His stationary haunt.

"Friend,"
I whisper   bending
my back as His back,
           Hanging   my head as His head,
slowly raising my hand
as He raises His twig-twisted hand.

Between my nearing-dawn bathroom trips we

Twist
Mirror
Twitch together:
 Friend,
 speak.
 Step toward me.

Outside, grass frosts and
cement cracks.
The Marchers rouse their howling trumpets,
sog leaves,
herald to the dying trees—
Knock one
Knock two
Knock three
against my screen door.

"Friend,
Speak to me."

Knock one
  Knock two
Knock three

Inside,
He mouths back
Friend,
Speak to me.
Blinks as I blink.

My eight-home town fills with Knocking
Frosting
Cracking
Sogging
Herolding.

"Who are they?"

He turns His head my eyes correct
to look like rotted fruit,
pussing and fly-burrowed.

"Who is in the School House?" I
ask, "Who is
the Maiden in the corn?"

He smiles to me
Or snarls to me
Or mocks me
and extends a crooked
cracking twig hand;
"Let me give you a tour."

On Your Knees, Dear Reader

Elk Grove Village

You are hunting or maybe you are camping,
it is too dark to tell and your car
is still running
with you sitting in the passenger seat.
The driver's seat is empty,
it has been empty a long time.
Your windshield is broken
and your buckle is still clipped in.

There is a man,
at least you think it's a man
with a face you forget every
Time you look away
standing outside your window.
His long crooked fingers draw omens
in the accumulating foggy glass.
He is speaking to you about his village.
A lovely village
the best of the best
and you see the moon peak over the pines
Only to hide again as she casts her
milky light over the man.

Your car door is open.
You don't remember opening it but
the bite of late summer's night

settles in your bones.
You shudder and the man smiles.
Perhaps smiling isn't right,
you don't remember him having lips
and then you remember nothing at all.

You unbuckle.
He steps back and holds out his hand,
the perfect gentleman.
You take it.

You don't remember stepping out of the car
The moon still refuses to come out.
Your feet have become bare.
Your legs are kissed by ferns and the downy hairs
of ancient foliage.
His body is lost to the darkness of the night,
the forest shadows swallow him.
His hand is the only source of lumination.
So is his head.
The thought comes so fleeting.
You crank your neck up to look to him and find
you do not know what you are looking at
and then voices
steal your attention.

Up ahead the forest is alight with warm
yellowed light.
Blazing pyred fire

crackles invitingly as elongated forms
dance around it.
Their tall shadows twist around tree trunks,
claw at the earth.

It smells like it's about to rain.

He announces your arrival with relish and
the forms you cannot quite distinguish into
recognizable parts— beyond
Knobby tree twig
Flash of pearly bone
Moss sticking to something dark—
usher you with their hands.
Hands like his.
Long and crooked.
You do not think they are human.
The hands comb through your hair
over your back
your arms
across your cheeks and eyes.
They guide you like the gentle tugging of
wind toward the fire, and there
at the foot of the pyre
is a platter of fruit.

"Eat.

Don't you want to remember us?"

The trees lining the pyre
are thick-trunked
Split open
from the ground to beyond the reach
of firelight,
like yawning mouths.
Fingers you know
in the dark corners of your
memory
twitch along the opening.
Their knobby knuckles give the yawning mouths
teeth
and the fruit smells so good.
One is open.
It wasn't open before
but now it spills
its juicy purple-red contents across the platter
dripping over the edge into the dirt.
You recognize you are meant to eat it mixed with soil.

You kneel as their hands smooth down your back
tangle your hair
brush your cheeks
cup your sides hungrily.
You squeeze the two halves of fruit.
They burn

the scrapes, glass-cuts, on your fingers.

You crashed your car.
The road was so lonely and—no
you were not camping
or hunting
or alone.
Something ran across the road
large and hunched over like an elk,
deformed front legs curled up
against it's cavernous chest.
Its face had been so white
So pearly
So eyeless
And you kept hitting a brake that would not stop
that would not give.

You were not alone.

You mix the pulp and runny skin of the fruit
into the dirt.
It is so warm.
The soil is alive.
You feel it breathe beneath your fingertips
and the voices keep saying
"Eat."

You will remember them.
They are all so tall
Their faces so...

How so?

"Eat."

The soil trembles
Recoils
as the last of the fruit melds muddily at your knees.

But back to the car.
You had been in a car
it had been yours
though now you cannot recall the color—
White like his face—
Or the make—
Crumpled against a tree like
Like who?—
Or the tires you worked two summers to customize
Or the groceries in the trunk,
you'd bought milk hadn't you?

"Eat" curls around your ear.

The soil is in your hands,
cupped and loose running like blood.
It is so close to your lips your tongue aches
with goosebumps.
The corners of your mouth drip
salivate.
You've lost your sight.
The fire has gone out.

The air is hotter than before,
Humid with breaths.
A single finger runs down your spine.
You know it
You have known it all your life
your mothe—

"Eat."

So you do.

The Hike that Breeds Desire

This one opens in Green.
His feet are hooved, clovered in
dark curling
fur.
There is a fragrance in the air you do not know,
or do not want to remember.
It stings the hair in your nose,
fires the nerves under your feet.

His hands are clawed, rusted with blood
gritty with mud.
One brushes your sunburnt sweating shoulder,
One curls around your neck.

You do not remember how you got to be so
Bare.
The breeze that rustles endless
green—bushes, weeds, trees—
blows through your bushes, your weeds.

The rocky path that you were hiking—
Yes, that's right,
You were hiking—
unfurles into a lush
cloven bed.
The leaves are lined thickly in Violet,

in dreary dreamy Blue,
slippery as the silver flash
of fish downstream.

His breath is hot, turning
summer's stagnant air sweltering.
Summer?
Was it summer when you
Left?
Where is your phone?
Where is your guide, your brother?

But the air is too hot to think
too hot to breathe,
and the fragrance is like something out of a
Dream.
It is familiar.
You have been here before.
You have been laid here and sown.

And his claws are like that of every
fainted faded
Lover.

I have known you since your first
Birth,
through your every spring
your every summer.
Since you swam out of every mother's waters.
I have known you from infancies
And every hour after.

The air is so hot
and the hour is so late—
When did it get to be so late?
The night is starless
Moonless
Lightless
and his breath keeps saying:

I have known you since your first
Birth,
through your every spring
your every summer
Since you swam out of every mother's waters.
I have known you from infancies
And every hour after.

And your phone—
Where is your phone?
Why does this night have no hour?
There are no crickets.
There are no croaking frogs
singing their loves songs.
There are no paths
no forsaken hiker's paths.

I have known you since your first
Birth,

And the fragrance is so familiar.

Through your every spring,

And his touch is like every fated
Fainted
Faded
Lover.

Your every summer,

And His hand has slipped to your
hip
His third hand
His fifth hand
His sixth,
Your eyes
Your lips
That sliver of a dip
high between your thighs.

He is so familiar
It is all

       so

          familiar.

I have known you, too
you hear yourself say.
In every garden sprig,
every hazy half-sleep blink.
Down the shadows of the hall.
Since my infancies,
my so many infancies.
I found you once, too,
in the fall.

Not me,
He replies
guiding you down into downy cloven
dreams.
Of me, of you.

In the Fall they find
You
dazed and confused
Beholding
a cloven-hooved child.

Moing'iima

Heavy come harvest
Heavy come harvest

The squash, they grow:
grow
drip
droop
drop
from his body.

Watermelon,
Corn,
Always sacred Corn,
hang
bloom
sprout
drip
droop
drop
from his body;
from the boy.

Heavy comes harvest.

He is full,
stooped
dragging

panting
sagging
with watermelon,
squash,
Corn
Always sacred Corn.

In the night he leaves drag marks
across your front door.
In the evening his breathless gasps
urge the wind to chill.

Heavy heavy–

In the mornings, sickles raised,
we sing:
heavy comes harvest heavy come–
as he collapses in the field, encircled
above by croning bloodied crows.

ReCreation

My garden is full of weeping,
my skies are starless.

Nightly, girls trench my flowerbeds
gasping
"Is that my lung? Is that your heart?"

Come dawn I wash their blood off
the cobalt stepping stones overrun
with weeds while fleet-footed foxes
pick their bones clean.
Through the open window She sings, satisfied.
Two new sprouts have come out of the ground today
baring used teeth riddled
in cavities.

In the kitchen a being with too many eyes
too many faces—*teeth*
flips flapjacks.
Window open,
She sings *"beloved belated*
the 'our ends
draped o'er weary women
baring bristled broches."
I come inside and kiss
her bruised bloody mouths,
relentless,

until the songbirds crawl out of the cellar
ready to hunt anew.

Yesterday She and I went berry picking.
I swallowed sticky berries that
fizzed as they crumbled
under my sharp teeth
and She sang about the end again;
the six black wren wings growing
out of her battered thorn-encircled head
twitching in glee.
The world is full of so much color
and half of it lives within her ten
too many fingers.

Tonight, more girls will come
tilling for the tactile taste
of their bodies,
and beloved-of-mine will have Her fill
and I will lay in bed,
pretending to sleep while lights whirl overhead,
heralding
in violent streaks of coppery-green.
Invisible trumpets will raise the dead
and leave them battered, begging on my chalky
salty doorstep.

All the while the little girls will whisper, witless
blind witnesses "is that my lung? Is that your liver?"
And my beloved—my beloved will tred
and tear
flesh from bone, precariously burying
their tiny teeth for tasteful tea leaves.

"What's it like
to live in your body?"
It's night. I stand in the kitchen
alone.
The girls are screaming and the day
seems so far away.
Where has the time gone?
Why has it always gone?
My shadow is in the doorway, carefully
out of the casted copper-green glow
I bathe in,
scorch in.
Distant drumbeats push a creek's dark flow
to the backdoor, lapping
licking the melting walls clean
I sound so much like a boy.
I could of sworn I was—
but maybe he—me—is a reminiscent
of the boys fertilizing my fields,
who's jaws and throat apples I found
with fonding
and added to my form.

"Like an invisible museum,"
I whisper "you could fill rooms
with all my stories—my bodies.
You could hang me upside down and
unroll my details
drop by drop.
Nail by nail.
The morning
The night
The end;
each flaked flesh a world.
I birth recreation,
team with it.
And She drags in the mixing parts
strip by fleshy strip
to decompose decompress
deatomaize under my palms."

The Corn Maiden

I made love once
in the twisting narrow passages
of a dying corn maze.

Lay,
She whispered to me
unfurling a quiet nook of soft
wet earth.

The late November night gave way
to the wild beating heating of summer—
to the field's secret heart;
breathing Her final moment of life into another.

Here,
Her voice curled.
Here,
Her leaves scraped,
scratched
into the deepest
folds of my skin.

Harbor me,
Her soil ran runny 'round my fingers
soaked through my yellow skirt.
Harbor the chance-thrown
love of your ancestors,
who bred me
to feed you.

I emerged at dawn
with Her dirt beneath my nails,
staining my soles,
burning life into my skin.

She has called to me every year—
Hundreds and hundreds of years after:
Every passing field of lush green
pyered in yellow combs bows wind-blown
toward me:
She lives in you
She lives in you
Mother Maiden is made anew.

I Found a Creature Seeking Death

Traversing the dim darkened wood there I came
upon a creature seeking death.

His back was arched as the blown over tree;
spin broken, burst as a beam. And stooped
over a bush of red berries His spindled fingers

                                                    plucked,

And there I stood
with my basket a-flow with blackened berries
until his fingers plucked no more.

What is it that he knows
that compels him to live no more?

They Speak Through the Trees

In the summer
height of Green
They come muffled,
near-silent
rattling through
the abandoned archaic garden's trees.

You strain to hear
the gnashing of teeth;
wispy wiry screams.
Nails knocking within
trees.

But when summer blows
into piles of Autumn's crunching leaves,
and the trees they go to sleep,
you hear Them
the gnashing of teeth:
Peel the wood
Peep within
Chant in threes— call our names
Set us free.

Stay away from the gnashing of teeth,
the slumbering trees,
the calls of *peel peep chant speak,*

the bark's crack that seeps sap so sweet,
the raw fleshy shavings of wood
sprinkling
down
Decaying trees

Marked

Thunder Comes Knocking

Rain shakes the foundations as She
comes to the door.

She's dressed in tears;
in the thousands of melting faces
She has touched.
The thousands of blood-clotted fashions She's ruined.
Coat after coat
Color after color
Face after Face.
Life
after
Life.

"Beloved,"
is the voice of thunder;
the voice that births life and
floods it.
She rapts Her knuckles against the door as
Coat
Color
Face
rumble off Her,
pooling in streaks of stringy pink on the porch.
It rolls thickly, cooly, under the door.

The keyhole becomes a fountain mouth;
running rusted red.
Your professor once said amazonian
floods are copper; so bright with minerals
life bursts at each touched drop.

Somewhere in your drafts
you have an email labeled for him
Life Does Not Burst It Drowns.

Your carpet floods,
stains.
The halls run like streams
screams
brushing your ankles in cold
crushing cascades.
That's another thing they don't tell you
life and death spring from the same thing:
Cold.

She knows you have woken, feels you struggle
—one foot in front of the other— through her flood
and remains
un-knocking at the door.

Your smile is running,
thawing into the rushing tide.
Your hands are shaking.
It is so much like drowning
your heart cannot tell the difference.
The knob slips and slips from under
your fumbling numbing thumbs.

"Allow me."
Her voice flows through the keyhole,
gentle, rocking with love.
It vibrates around your ankles.
Bubbles deep in the basement,
in the fluid chambers of your heart.

The lock breaks under water weight.

Your life runs away from you:
Couch swept out the back door.
A floating pizza box, still warm, slips
through the open window.
Your forgotten keys become entangled in loose
cords.
Your clothing dissolves.
The family photos
heirlooms
decorates
dinner plates
drift away.

All your life has lived indoors,
in waiting.

"Beloved,"
You step out to greet Her
with a kiss.

A Different Dusk

The Spirit of spring has left
Us.
Behold,
on comes the colorful march of the dead.

Community Center

He roams the halls
Soaked in red light
School converted community center
Converted
Unresting place
For the boy.

In the nights he plays
On the swings
Swaying
Up down up down up down u—
In the still air.

I want to swing beside him
What is your name?
Do you long for a friend?

But Those That Live in the Woods
Watch
And even the grass to which I call
For protection
Can only do so much to keep
Them at bay
So close to the Wood's edge.

Spoken Through the Drippy Backroom Faucet

It's time you face me.

I've woken every moment your
friends scream Take
         a peek. Take
               a sneak
        and
you
press your muddy brown eye
against the keyhole.
The sheeted lumps stored within the attic move,
footfalls scraping.

You know you've seen too much.
The floor is stained with their hunger,
      Our hunger.

I am there every moment your parents say
stay safe
drive safe
with their perfectly unsafe smiles,
thinking you oblivious to the attic;
your heirloom.
And you grab the car keys
swallowed after swallowed shot,
shaking

breaking yourself into the lie— *the drive will be enough,*
the drive will be enough thedrivewillbe—

enough

enough

enough.

       I've seen nothing.

At prom you tried to kiss me
stuffed in a darkened gym
shower.
Our breaths came the same
in out
in out
as your thumb brushed our feathered
scars.
Our sheets were left discarded, stuffed
down between the lockers.
Our cheeks were so flushed, so red
left forgotten the dripping of blood.
Hunger in us, all of us, is the same.

Four years ago you grabbed a shovel
and buried me in the yard.
Wrapped in twine,
smeared in rowanberry paste,
pyred by brittle
brittle
cinnamon sticks.

So I humored you,
as love most deprived
does.

I waited
by the fuzzy corner of your sight,
in the flash of oncoming
headlights,
in your mirrored reflection
as you wash dish
after
dish.
Obedient wife.
Doesn't that notation
drive you wild?
How did you become this way?
How did you get to be so old?

And now,
you hear me once more.
Come.
Peel the
wallpaper.
Splitter the beams,
Light the fires.
Call our true name,
All our names.

The faucet drips as you dry
dish after dish.

You were always me and I
was always part of
You.

Remember the kiss?

You resist.
Your husband is in the dining room
smoking
as the radio voices blur.

This is your life.

Stuffed away into your role
you live smothered
in smoke
hoping the foul scent
will mask me away— mask
You away.

The yellow light above your head might as well be a
rusted halo.

The radio blurs
The stranger smokes
The lumps move
The wallpaper peels
and the beams split and
that kiss that kiss—
"Marco."

"Polo," I reply
and the lights go out.

Water Whispers

There are times in the darkest
folds of night
when you will hear the chatter
of many voices
lapping
laughing
trilling— trickling
into one another through the pipes,
in the lone toilet flush,
breaking sound sleep.

And you will understand,
for you have been marked since birth
and again marked Wed
under each loving rainfall kiss,
the secrets we have all told:

in the shower	or your cat's fountain bow
to the river	between walls sticky with humidity
coughed into the well	cried down into the rain drains

whispered into the sprinkle of a hose.

All voices One
through Me.

What'll become of the barn?   *Do you think he loves me?*
I saw a hoofed rider.   *The wallpaper feels like an itch.*
I'm not a boy.   *I murdered her I murdered her*
                                         I—
Where am I? Why is it so cold?

But

if you are kind,
and you are not always kind
you will get down on your sullen soggy
knees
water swamping your bathroom floor
and whisper back into the bowl:
In water there is no emptiness.
When I die I will become water, become
you
at all points in time.
For all of us who speak to water
are a part of water and will become
water,
not blow away rusted like ash.

Grant Me the Gift to Unsee

Rust and moths cling
to the torn edges of your dress.
The streep lamps flicker:
Yellow white yellow white yellow–
light stings my sleepless eyes
as I wait draped
in cast iron and fox fur
for your nightly return.

What wouldn't mortals give
to catch a glimpse
of your tattered form,
flaking and fleshing
tapping upon every blood-marked
door?
What wouldn't I give
to get your sordid serenading song
and decomposing courting gifts
off my porch.

The Marchers

At night they come chanting
Come see,
Come See.
Their feet leave frost
crack cement
sog leaves
kill fleas.

Come see,
Come see.

At night they come knocking
Speak with me.

Windows shudder
shake
pots shatter and
break.
Your screen door comes open,
hinges splintering, and they
Knock   One
Knock   Two
Knock   Three

I know   your mother
I know   your father
I know your every wanton desire.

I know wheather it will all end in ice
or in fever,
                    or
in the reluctant prophet's singing dream.

They knock,
grey boned fingers rapting
on every decaying winter's tree,
waking
They who Speak Through the Trees.

Avert All Mortal Eyes

Home

The door opens,
creaking.
You can smell the rust coming off the hinges
like fresh blood.

The night has arisen twisted—
Moonless
Starless.

Your childhood halls smell like winter:
The beginning of christmas,
gingerbread cookies.
That nasty cinnamon candle
your father ran from
and your mother lit
like a victory.

Your feet—too big
—for the papaya rug
at the foot of your bunk bed
curl
in the dusty fabric.

There is old rosemary hidden under your pillow.
You used to eat one leaf a night,
puking your father's genes out of you

while your mother spent her nights
with an ear pressed to the bathroom door,
hoping.

Your top bunk was always empty,
to adults.
In the twilight you would watch
pale boney feet—
toes not fully formed—
dangle over the side of the top mattress
and
             wiggle
until you couldn't feel your skin.
And in the dawn,
when your mother slept and your father
roamed
the feet would slip,
weighted,
and a body unformed would splatter
all over your bright orange papaya rug.

Your feet
fully formed
now curl and claw at the rug.
The door is still opening.
The soles of your feet are oozing
warmth
sucking up all that was yours

and that you denied yourself
for petty morality.

Your father comes in with a black trash bag
weighted
sloshing.
It drags along the same floor you
dressed your dolls on.
Soundless,
he opens it.

"Your birthright."

You spent so many nights
performing exorcisms on yourself
in the mirror.
So many dawns burying yourself alive
in the yard.
So many birthdays baking rosemary
into your cakes and stabbing your palms
with stakes.
Your father pulls a hair tie out of his pocket
and you
you
you

"Partake."

School House

To speak of her
is to risk her summoning
out from between the heavy
sun-stripped logs
of the settler's schoolhouse,

and her prison stands far
too close
One
Door
Down
to risk her escape.

But if we were to speak of her—
It would be of the way her breath fogs
the dusty paned glass
exerting heat deep in the slumberous winter,
and how her nails bite
the cracked chalkboard
at the start of each school year
The cat is orange
The sun is yellow
The gold finch watches from the shrine—
I am a good pupil

a good pupil a good pupil a good pu

The Motel on Briery Branch

"Do you have the materials?"

You're both standing in a dirty motel, squat and slanting—roof
moss-eaten—on the edge of the ~~⬛~~ National Park. The one-lane
highway remains silent, streetlamps burnt out decades ago. Lane dividers glint
soft orange as the moon curls its rays loose from looming black woods.

Somewhere, hundreds of miles away, Your boy
friend lays crumpled—decomposing—
in someone's beat-up beige truck.
Somewhere, hundreds of inches away, Your boy
friend's killer lays lumpy—head concave—
clotted blood stuck to the road like tar.
Your hands still vibrate from the rumble of the engine:
Forward, reverse, forward, reverse *reverse reverse re*—
until head and hair melded flat, smoothly
fitted against the poorly paved road.

    "Hey, Andrew, are you listening?"

It had taken You by the hand, head split double, eyes as hollow as the road
was dark with Your kill's blood.
        It had come crawling out

                  speckled
                  and smiling with gray matter;
                  a starved god pleased.

"Andrew?"

You're arranging teeth
twigs
    creekbed pebbles
        the papery bodies of mayflies
onto the cracked yellow sink, leading a bridal path down to the tub.
"Yeah, listening."
Listening, pulling the dark leather shift into *reverse*
reverse reverse.

Twin owls lay stiff
on the tiled bathroom floor
speckled white, grey, a blooming pink.
It had brought them before You
as You sat by the road, watching flies gather.
The hunger in You was so deep.
"Good boy," *It* had said, "Raise me the Appalachian dead."

And so now You set fat white pillar candles along the rim of the tub.
With a snap they all ignite reeking of sulfur, rot.
Your fingertips sting.

The rusted sink knob turns on its own,
loud
aching,
flooding the basin with brackish water

The moonlight cautiously watching
through broken windows and crumbled plaster fails
as You take off your socks   and slice
the bottom of Your feet
with a coffin nail,
shuddering.
Water surges–hungry, starved–towards You
dying itself pink in Your blood.

It has left You, fleeing for dryer ground.

You take the first owl with bare fingers reaching, deepening, through the
parted beak.
"I bring you twin deaths," You face the mirror, staring at the black figure
standing behind You in the splintering reflection. He smiles and You
falter. You had not expected Your exorcized ex.

"Owls dressed in feathered freedom be now of your sacred flock." He preens
and You remember the way those claws felt scraping
the column of Your throat.
 "Grant me
        their eyes, grant me
                    their ears,
to sense the Old sleeping and pluck
them swiftly to waking with my shovel."

In the mirror Your eyes have turned black. You squeeze them shut and jerk

Your hand in the owl, turning it inside out with a wet snap.

Cracked feathers stick to your palms and You

think You remember what it was like to be stripped of Your wings.

The same stench, the same snap.

       as you feast I feast."

You push the bird deep into the sink—far deeper than the sink should go—as

a clawed hand brushes your own, *wanting,* and pulls the owl

deep

down.

In the mirror, He holds the owl in one hand, the other pointed toward the bathtub

where the second owl lays.

You ghost a strange pattern on Your lips, fingertips black where the creature has touched You.

You keep

your eyes on the mirror as you take one step back–then another–removing

shirt, pants, underwear with each step. He

crosses His arms along the edge of the mirror, all torn lips parted.

The room is suddenly too hot.

Your calves bump the tub, frigid,

and with eyes still on the mirror You climb inside.

Dark hot liquid oozes over the edge, snuffing white candles into black.

"Consume,"

is the voice of shattering glass,
the breaking of bones, the final frustrated frayed vocal cord
of desperation;
the infliction of language plucked taunt,
unused to human sounds.
It comes from everywhere, rippling the water on the floor.

You hold the second owl in Your hands. You don't remember picking it up,
You don't remember breaking it open in half   like an apple;
its white ribs an inviting basket,
holding warm organs like an offering.

Your breathing's too loud, too calm. It falls out in white puffs in the hot room
as You lift the owl to Your face   *whimpering*
 and slurp the carcass clean of intestines.

In the mirror He does the same,
red
    spilling
          down
His shadowy frame. Grooved scales, rough patterned like the demons of old,
glow
painted in the thick slow-dripping blood.

As the last organ slides down Your throat
the lights snap on.
The candles blow out, leaving no smoke trail. All the water, blood,
gore—owls—gone.

It's just You kneeling naked in the tub, gripping *grasping* for dear life as You
repeatedly
gag and swallow
        swallow and gag,
tears stinging down Your face
like the bite of a promise ring.

The Gun Chest

I see him reflected in glassdoors
luminous
in the night,
waving three
bent grey fingers.

I stare ahead,
breath even.

Sometimes it's best
they not know you
See.

Accidental Arrangement

It stands in the doorway, teeth bared,
cicadas screaming—choiring—in slow growing winter.
It shakes sloshing chocolatey liquid
across the blisteringly bright
oxidized orange door
oil seeping like dark rivers between the grooves,
staining old ragged bird scratches.

You're sit in the car, watching It's—His— form;
hands shifting into claws   shifting back   to soft onyx
nubs
and you think about the axe in the trunk,
the gun in the glove compartment,
the

          way

                    dawn
broke out of a restless snowy pre-morning blue
hours ago as you   and He   laid unsleeping,
motel sheets crinkling, as traveler's arguments floated un-muted
between cardboard painted walls.
The graveyard still clung to your boots then—strapped around
your twisted ankles.
His face had fanned with blood, eyes hazily lusted
over your since-healed heart.
You wish He'd met His end under your shovel,
or that graves were shallower.

But demons are hard to kill,

"*Extended life demands sacrifice,*"

And now there He paces, lighter in claw— hand
framed by the red, blue, green   christmas morning
and the quiet poinsettia-lined street.

Inside your neighbor is screaming.
          Bound and gagged, nails pulled and neatly   arranged
          into old numbers, sly jagged symbols on the porch.
Cicadas choir to his terror
sweetened, drowned, melodized by their ear-splitting joy.
The sparking heat of the basement, first floor,
front door
          kindles them against icicle-framed trees.

He slips into the passenger seat   singing hell-songs
as you fix the rear mirror, smiling bitter
at your own stinging sun-warped face.
                    "*Extended life demands sacrifice,*"
And who better than your photogenic neighbor
with his hidden bedside table
brimming
with too small not yet able fingers
and legs?

Hour of the Bees

On the banks of Plum Creek
sways
the sweetest sound:
river magic,
root magic,
the soft sighed decomposition of the dead.

The humming yellow-and-black stars of summer
paint the wind
as flowers rise and wilt
wilt and rise
under the yolky sunny sky.

The flies arrive like locus
—buttery iridescent cleaners, eaters—
as I stand above you.

    Chewing and spitting
    spitting and chewing,
    grooming   twitching   swarming
    feasting.
    Their feet groove against your teeth,
    their wings flutter your clumpy eyelashes.

How long have we been on this bank?
I above you drinking the bees and the river
and you,

                still
dewy   with dried red
crumbling quietly with rot.

You sigh—a fittingly feeble final goodbye—as
your lung collapses, collides,
with Holy vultured claws.
          And   I   remember how that used to feel
against my thigh.

The hot noon air is rife with life;
the sweet sound of river babble,
the slow stretching excavating hunger
of roots bringing flowers
to bloom
under the pale blued moons of your nails.
And   *at last*   my eyes   unclouding, muscles
unclamping—slow from their time below ground.
And   *at long last*   my heart restarting
resurrecting
Reviving.

The Equinox

There's a man in the corn fields whistling
while the ladies scutter through the stirring stalks
blindfolded.
The rough fabric flakes their reddened skin
as their fingers curl deftly 'round
ear after ear, dropping
squashing pussing fruit
into lamenting wicker baskets
while the stinging stalk leaves protest and curl
–stretching, scratching–
trying to wrench their eyes free.

You stand, idly, the only lady (?)
dressed fit for a groom.
If anyone was to decided, declaim, dictate
you a Him not Her not They
it would be *The Him*, The Man In The Fields.

The woman call each other's names:
> Clark
> Clandestite
> Calamity
> Renee
> Tamaray

And each call falls shorter than the last:

                    Clark
                    Clandestite
                    Calamity
                    Renee?

The hay man demands his equinox prize;
a groom, a bride—
this year it's the ladies who cry
through the fields averting their eyes.

Crisp autumnal air bites you
peeling dry
what was not left horse of your voice
shouting
"I am not a bride, I am not a *bride*."
But you are—most want to be—a groom.

                    Clark
                    Clandestite
                    Calamity
                    Calamity!
                    For the love of god Calam—

The stalks stir and sigh
parting ways on either side
as the hushed soft scratching

of footed hay passing—pauses
by your side.

C-Clark?
Clandestine?

You had seen Him the year before last
fresh and weakened   fallen
from prime after harvest.
His vestments had torn old
Patch-needed by The Maiden
who had forsaken watch of our field
of corn and bred Him
scare-crowed skinned walker.

Clark?
Clark!

"And what do they call you?"
The voice is a fever   itching
your face, brains, veins.

Oh *god finch* please please CLAR—
"Clark."

A hand slides crinkling
pleasing sun-dried beetles through
your cheeks, scalp, heart.

*"Oh, I see. How would you like to be
my Man of the Hearth?"*

Awaken

This is What the Trumpets Sound Like at the End of Everything

Come in an absent dream,
at the edge of the world.
The giver of stars calls upon
Night
Sleep
Death,
The Neighbor.

The summer-water
you
drowned in
whispers softly
Come, tumbling
          down

               deep?
No,   *up.*

Waker, throw yourself at
the Corn Maiden
The Marchers
your Father—the fern-laying beast—
while a fever of bones grips all
crawling bloodied in the streets.
Desperation does not listen

to those in its grasp;
the trumpets do not cease.

If you want to make the First God—silent
little watching finch—laugh
say
You are cold hearted,
as you lay frozen stiff
along the river's bend
mending
sordid wound after
sordid wound.
His feathers will flutter golden
like giggles.

                              The weight of a life
                                so water-logged
                              was a heavy one;
                              do not disappoint us.

The wreckage of this town will see you to
Her, for you
are Her beloved night bed-guest,
spawn of the Hike that Breeds.

The bodies in the birches will call,
bemoaning
warning you

of the man without a shadow;
quiet deep-night rider.
On a hoof-less horse he
looks for you, calling
Reluctant prophet sing,
unashamed sing.

We are not ourselves,
forgive us.

At the end of the world
the giver of stars calls upon
Night
Death
Sleep
The Neighbor
and you will answer the call
—Friend, speak—
crawling desperately out of the lake
you drowned in
two years, eight months,
and twenty eight days ago.

Night, Death, Sleep, The Neighbor

It is cold when You wake.
The morning has not yet risen
and Your town lays tucked
in pre-bird silence, cradled between far reaching mountains.

Summer calls the return of the gold finch,
silent stalker of gardens and powerlines.
You see him creep along the window box
—luring morning glories to blossom—
while You kneel in damp carpet.
Your lungs feel so full.
The night must have been hot, Your sleep
restless,
to tangle in such strange dreams and find
refuge on the floor.

You do not remember the house being so old,
the walls so peeling,
the lightbulbs so moth filled,
the window so dusted.
When had Your nail beds gone so purple?

It could not have been more than two
hours—maybe three—since You rose
for the restroom, husband forgotten asleep,
and met...

The gold finch taps, impatient, his wings dandelions
heralding the summer.
Beyond Your brick walls a fire siren moans lowly,
pulling the lightest town sleepers from slumber, and
You get the strangest nagging wonder that the morning
sounds like heralding hungry trumpets.

Coming 2026

Follow a cross-country traveling paranormal specialist struggling to find his place at the end of the universe, as the stars die out one by one.

Read an exclusive sneak peek!

Allow Me to Introduce You...to You

How long have you been standing there?
Fragment after fragment   after   fragment
   broken
between dark plum-tender eyes,
cupid lips split *runny* like dark rivers trickle
through chipped rock.

The dying overhead bulbs—yellowed and buzzing—are praying
hymns
for Beelzebub their lord.
And don't you feel rotted enough for the feast already?
The flies are close to swarming,
legs tapping *incessant*
clawed hooves doubled in the mirrored glass.

Little prey, why do you run?
Do you not tire?
The universe has grown smaller.
You've run out of worlds to hide in
and yet *still* you go— drive aimless:
dive bar
gas station
crumbling motels stained old
with blood from torn open runners
just like you.

When did your life stop being your own?   You tumble in the bottle,
Was it when the stars started to go out,   bounce
one by one, then ton after ton?   between line dividers and road signs.

Was it your first *demonic* kiss?

The surrounding bulbs blow out   Uh-oh, memory calls to master.
and your face is left echoing,   highlighted hollow   under the last beam of yellow
in a chasm of slow flushing toilets.

You can feel the kiss now still, can't you?   Wet warm lips opening like a wound,
What did He promise you?   each movement bloodier than the last.
Was it lasting love?

Power?

The single light flickers, leaving seconds empty of you.
The dark is a welcomed place to hide,
but prey does not stay concealed forever.

You push His memory aside and the light snaps on
like an opening eye.

                              Do you see me?
                          Something dispersed
                       in the muggy Georgia day.
             No. Of course not.
Instead,
You
    think
       was
    the gap between your front teeth always so pronounced?
It's a cavern you don't see yourself through
   Endless
A space between what is You   and   what is nothing but empty air.
You want to fold inside
crumple in it
like a spider pulled through a vacuum.

You want good food
You want sleep
You want to *run.*

They're catching up.
Who knows how long now
before the Lords and their dogs
catch scent.
You've stayed too still.
The reflection bares your scarred face,
hollow with fear and calling
to its master.
The gasoline pumps outside won't hide
your stench forever— flesh burned through
with brimstone.
Your blood is a sparked match for hungry
twisted things.

Behind you a stall opens, clattering like hoof beats.
Hadn't that stall been empty?
"Empty?"
"Hey man," the voice echoing in the dark is twisted, smiled
teeth sharp— *starved.*
 "You done yet? Your blood's filling up the sink."

First published by Haunted Words Press, December 2024

Acknowledgements

My infinite gratitude goes to the literary magazines, reviews, and presses who first brought the following poems into the eyes of the world:

"Elk Grove Village" first published in Crow & Cross Keys (August, 2022).

"The Hike that Breeds Desire" first published in Crow & Cross Keys (September, 2022).

"Moing'iima" first published in The Horror Zine (April, 2023)

"ReCreation" first published in Crow & Cross Keys (April, 2023)

"The Corn Maiden" first published in Prismatica Press' anthology *They Came From the Closet* (October, 2022) under the pen name Damian Alba Craft.

"I Found a Creature Seeking Death" first published in Black Poppy Review (April, 2022)

"They Speak Through the Trees" first published in Black Poppy Review (April, 2022)

"Thunder Comes Knocking" first published in The Horror Zine (April, 2023)

"Community Center" first published in The Horror Zine (April, 2023)

"Grant Me the Gift to Unsee" first published in Prismatica Press' anthology *They Came From the Closet* (October, 2022) under the pen name Damian Alba Craft.

"Home" first published in Crow & Cross Keys (July, 2022).

"Hour of the Bees" first published in Panorame Press' *The Gothic Summer* (June, 2023).

In *Night Life*'s first six months of life it has been nominated for the following awards and received the following honors:

Science Fiction & Fantasy Poetry Association 2024 Elgin Award

2023 Queer Indie Awards
Best Horror
Best Poetry
Best Debut
Best Dark Fantasy
Best World Building

2023 Indieverse Awards
Best Poetry Book
Most Creative Layout
Most Cinematic Writing
Favorite Book to Read in the Dark

Featured Book at the 2024 Gaithersburg Book Festival
Featured Authorat the 2024 Gaithersburg Book Festival

I want to express my profoundest thanks to my readers. Without your love for this book these nominations and honors would not have been possible.

About the Author

Alba Sarria is a poet and flash fictionist fascinated by all things eerie, disquieting, and romantically entangled in folklore. You can usually find Alba wandering old cemeteries at night, fulfilling dying wishes for the dead, and keeping flower-less graves company.

Alba is the 2018 Columbia Scholastic Press Association Gold Circle Award winner for Free Form Poetry, the 2021 Gold Circle CM for short fiction, the 2021 William Heath Award recipient, the 2021 First Place winner of Polaris' Fiction Competition, and a 2022 Pushcart nominee.

To contact Alba, fog your bathroom mirror at 4:13am and write their name backwards in blood. All inquiries and gossip will be replied to through cryptic temperature changes, hall light flickering, and sudden toilet flushing. Or, you can give Alba a follow on Instagram: @albasarriawrites

MONSTROUS LOVE LOUNGE
PRESS

Available paperback version published by Monstrous Love Lounge Press. For more information visit monstrousloveloungepress.com